Cougar
The Musical

Book and Lyrics
Donna Moore

Music
Donna Moore, Meryl Leppard,
Mark Barkan, Arnie Gross, John
Baxindine, and Seth Lefferts

Additional Lyrics
Meryl Leppard
and Mark Barkan

A SAMUEL FRENCH ACTING EDITION

FOUNDED 1830

SAMUELFRENCH.COM
SAMUELFRENCH-LONDON.CO.UK

FOR PRODUCTION ENQUIRIES

UNITED STATES AND CANADA
Info@SamuelFrench.com
1-866-598-8449

UNITED KINGDOM AND EUROPE
Plays@SamuelFrench-London.co.uk
020-7255-4302

Each title is subject to availability from Samuel French, depending upon country of performance. Please be aware that *COUGAR THE MUSICAL* may not be licensed by Samuel French in your territory. Professional and amateur producers should contact the nearest Samuel French office or licensing partner to verify availability.

MUSIC USE NOTE

Licensees are solely responsible for obtaining formal written permission from copyright owners to use copyrighted music in the performance of this play and are strongly cautioned to do so. If no such permission is obtained by the licensee, then the licensee must use only original music that the licensee owns and controls. Licensees are solely responsible and liable for all music clearances and shall indemnify the copyright owners of the play(s) and their licensing agent, Samuel French, against any costs, expenses, losses and liabilities arising from the use of music by licensees. Please contact the appropriate music licensing authority in your territory for the rights to any incidental music.

RENTAL MATERIALS

An orchestration consisting of **Piano/Vcoal Score** and **Drums** will be loaned two months prior to the production ONLY on the receipt of the Licensing Fee quoted for all performances, the rental fee and a refundable deposit. Please contact Samuel French for perusal of the music materials as well as a performance license application.

IMPORTANT BILLING AND CREDIT REQUIREMENTS

If you have obtained performance rights to this title, please refer to your licensing agreement for important billing and credit requirements.

COUGAR THE MUSICAL was opened Off-Broadway at the St. Luke's Theatre in New York City on August 12, 2012. The performance was directed by Lynne Taylor-Corbett, with sets and lights by Josh Iacovelli and costumes by Dustin Cross. . The Production Stage Manager was Susan Whelan. The cast was as follows:

LILY . . . . .Catherine Porter

MARY-MARIE. . . . . .Babs Winn

CLARITY . . . . Brenda Braxton

BUCK. . . . . Danny Bernardy

CHARACTERS

LILY – In her late forties. She is attractive, naive, and emotionally wounded. but possessing an inner strength and confidence waiting to be unleashed.

MARY-MARIE – In her fifties. She is a Southern gal, full of life with innate comic timing.

CLARITY – In her forties or fifties. She is African American or Hispanic. Her determined, opinionated and rigid demeanor masks an underlying 'joie de vivre'.

BUCK – In his twenties. He is handsome, athletic, smart, an old soul, and wiser than his years. This actor plays multiple characters: **EVE**, an Asian manicurist, **TWILIGHT DUDE, BOURBON COWBOY, GOLIATH, 'CATSABLANCA' BARTENDER** and **NAKED PETER**.

SETTING

A 'cosmopolitan city' near you.
(Feel free to adapt references of local newspapers and magazines to accommodate locale.)

TIME

Now

AUTHOR'S NOTES

This piece is written to be approached with sincerity and seriousness, allowing the pathos and humor of the material to be easily mined by the actor.

– Donna Moore, Author/Lyricist/Composer

COUGAR THE MUSICAL is performed in one act and runs approximately ninety minutes.

DIRECTOR'S NOTES

COUGAR is a wonderful vehicle for challenging stereotypes without playing them. It is the story of three unique women who individually find themselves at a turning point. As they strike out to reinvent their lives, attempting to become what they imagine men want, their heartfelt sincerity provides the basis for the humor. The more honest the performances, the more fun the audience has.

The scenic elements can be very simple. In the original production, the bar area was very far stage right, the park bench and street light very far left; both remained throughout. A chaise lounge was rolled on to represent Mary-Marie's office/"boudoir", three small tables and rolling stools, along with a rolling cart loaded with supplies represented the beauty parlor. The scenic movement was choreographed for actors and deck hands. In order make a clean look in a relatively small space, I color-keyed each scene, for instance shiny red for Eve's Nail Salon, pinks for the boudoir, deep purple for the bar. Very specific lighting helped greatly with the storytelling.

It was tremendously fulfilling to hear cascades of laughter and then some gasps and even tears toward the end of the show. It is a richly diverse piece and I wish you a wonderful time with it!

–Lynne Taylor-Corbett
Director/Choreographer

SONG LIST

On The Prowl (LILY, MARY-MARIE, CLARITY)
Swagger (BUCK)
I'm My Own Queen (CLARITY)
Gary's Right (LILY)
The Cougar (LILY, TWILIGHT DUDE, MARY-MARIE)
Shiny and New (CLARITY, MARY-MARIE, LILY and EVE)
Say Yes (CLARITY, MARY-MARIE, LILY)
Let's Talk About Me (BUCK, LILY)
Julio (CLARITY)
I'm Easy (LILY)
My Terms (MARY-MARIE)
Mother's Love (MARY-MARIE, LILY)
Love is Ageless (LILY, BUCK)
At The End of the Day (MARY-MARIE, CLARITY, LILY, BUCK)

Love is ageless...

Prologue, Fantasy Disco

(Three powerful women in slick raincoats and sunglasses appear in a fantasy sequence and proceed to 'hit on' imaginary young men, in a highly choreographed number.)

[MUSIC: No. 1 – "ON THE PROWL"]

CLARITY.
HISS

ALL THREE WOMEN.
MEOW

LILY. Protect your children, there's Cougars in the club!

MARY-MARIE. I'm gonna get that young bear cub!

CLARITY. Check out the prey at five o'clock! I'll chat him up, then load and lock!

ALL THREE WOMEN
AAGH, AAGH…. AAGH, AAGH, AAGH

CLARITY. Nice ass!

ALL THREE WOMEN.
AAGH, AAGH…. AAGH, AAGH, AAGH

(All three women start strutting like Janet Jackson in "What Have You Done For Me Lately?")

I BET YOU WANNA DANCE A MILE IN MY SHOES
I MEAN, I CUT THE RUG REAL GOOD
I'M IN CONTROL AND I GOT NOTHING TO LOSE

CLARITY.
EXCEPT MY INHIBITION

MARY-MARIE.
CAUSE I HAVE FOUND MY MISSION

LILY.
AND NOW I KNOW HE'S WISHIN'
HE COULD HAVE A LITTLE BIT A SUMPIN', SUMPIN'

CLARITY/LILY.
SUMPIN', SUMPIN'
ALL THREE WOMEN.
SUMPIN', SUMPIN' GOOD ENOUGH FOR ME-E-E!
MARY-MARIE. Come here often?
LILY. I'll sleep when I am in my coffin.
ALL THREE WOMEN.
I SEE HE'S WATCHING ME SASHAY 'CROSS THE FLOOR
PILATES HELPS WITH GRAVITY
THESE LAST TEN YEARS HAVE MADE ME THIRSTY FOR MORE
LILY.
SO GET THE RED BULL GOING
CLARITY.
MAKE SURE THE WINE IS FLOWING
MARY-MARIE.
IS THAT YOUR THONG THAT'S SHOWING?
HE COULD HAVE A LITTLE BIT OF SUMPIN' SUMPIN'
CLARITY/MARY-MARIE.
SUMPIN' SUMPIN'
ALL THREE WOMEN.
SUMPIN' SUMPIN' GOOD ENOUGH FOR ME-E-E!
IT'S FUN TO ASSUAGE THIS MIDLIFE WE WAGE
BUT LIFE'S TOO SHORT SO LET'S HOOT AND HOWL
GET ON THE SAME PAGE, IT'S TIME TO ENGAGE!
MARY-MARIE. Just don't ask my age when I'm…
ALL THREE WOMEN.
ON THE PROWL, ON THE PROWL, ON THE PROWL!
AAGH, AAGH…. AAGH, AAGH, AAGH
CLARITY. I won't bite
ALL THREE WOMEN.
AAGH, AAGH…. AAGH, AAGH, AAGH
CLARITY. Hard!
LILY.
THE OLDER I BECOME THE YOUNGER I FEEL
MARY-MARIE.
IT'S GOOD I'VE LEARNED A THING OR TWO

CLARITY.

NOW I'M A DIVA WHO'S JUST LEARNING TO HEAL
SO HERE'S THE DEAL WE'LL SPEAK ON

MARY-MARIE.

I'LL LET YOU SLAP MY CHEEK, HON

LILY.

TONIGHT WE'LL GET OUR FREAK ON
AND HE'LL HAVE A LITTLE BIT OF SUMPIN' SUMPIN'

CLARITY/LILY.

SUMPIN' SUMPIN'

ALL THREE WOMEN.

SUMPIN' SUMPIN'
GOOD ENOUGH FOR ME-E-E!
LIFE IS THE RAGE IN MENAPAUSE STAGE
BUT I'M TOO YOUNG TO THROW IN THE TOWEL
I'M OUT OF MY CAGE
A MODERN DAY SAGE
Just don't ask my age!!! When I'm…
ON THE PROWL, ON THE PROWL, ON THE PROWL,

CLARITY.

ON THE PROWL

ALL THREE WOMEN.

WE'RE ON THE PROWL! ROAWR!

(Cross fade to Street,"ON THE PROWL" underscore.)

*(***BUCK*** crosses on his way to the Elder Grille and Younger Boys Lounge. He stops to check the street address on his iPhone and hurries on.)*

[MUSIC: No. 1A – "ON THE PROWL PLAYOFF"]

Scene One. Church Basement, Room F

(LILY comes running into a support group. Under her trench coat, she is dressed like Dorothy from The Wizard of Oz.)

LILY. Excuse me, is this basement room F? *"Over Forty and Fabulous"*? Sorry, didn't mean to interrupt. My work went overtime. I can come back next week. Oh, Okay, thanks, I'll just sit down and listen in.

Uh, me? Well, hi…my name is Lily and I'm 'Over Forty and Fabulous'. Things are good. My twin daughters went off to the same college last September and they're both really happy – which is the point, right? People used to say *'empty nest'* and I'd think, "What the hell is that"? I mean, I'm finally free! Jeez, it's hot in here.

(She takes off her coat to reveal a Dorothy outfit.)

I should explain. I'm a children's birthday party entertainer…this is my *Dorothy* from *The Wizard of Oz*. It's very popular with gay couples who adopt. And luckily, kids are still getting older despite the economy so I've been skipping down the yellow brick road a lot lately. Katching! So actually, I'm good. I don't even know why I'm here.

(She gets up to leave and sits back down.)

Actually I do. My divorce papers came in today. As soon as I sign them and mail them back to the lawyer, it'll be final. Finito! Why'd he leave me? It was my decision to file for divorce but it's only because he'd already left me. At least, in the ways that *mattered*. I'm rambling but I just don't see a way out of this conundrum. And now I feel old and tired and shriveled up. Hell, I'm thinking of starting a new social media site called '*Facelift Book*'. Oh God, I'm nothing but an aging trophy wife…

[MUSIC: No. 1B – "THE WIZARD OF LILY"]

LILY. *(cont)* …in a ridiculous costume…talking to strangers about divorce papers. Wishing I could just click my heels and disappear!

(She pivots and runs out to 'The Wicked Witch of the West' theme. Blackout.)

Scene Two. Clarity's Office

(**CLARITY** *paces the floor while proofreading a letter she has written.*)

CLARITY.

'Dear Mr. White,

While I have enjoyed my twenty-year run as Senior Financial Analyst for *Who-Can-You-Trust, Inc.*, I have spent the last thirty-nine months, three days, four hours and thirty-three minutes volunteering at The Women's Crisis Center. And it has changed me. I want… no –

(*She picks up her pen to edit.*)

I *NEED* to understand the underlying angst that is present for women of all colors and demographics in America today? *How can we reclaim our innate sacred power?*

Ergo, I enrolled in night classes at NYU, and must now prepare my thesis for a graduate degree. Therefore, I regret to inform you'… Aw, scratch that. HONEY, I QUIT!

(*She crumples up the letter and throws it on the desk.*)

I thought all these years I was giving people *steam for their dreams* but now I see I was just one more *cook for your books*!

(*She grabs a paper fan and fans herself furiously.*)

Oh, dear Lord, now I'm hot flashing.

[MUSIC: No. 2 – "I'M MY OWN QUEEN"]

(*Reggae music in.*)

Mama, I sure hope you were right when you said…

BE A LADY THAT MAKES HER OWN RULES
WHETHER YOU'RE THIN OR FAT, YOU'LL OWN THE JEWELS
DON'T BE NO FRAIDY CAT CUZ FEAR IS FOR FOOLS
MAMA KNEW WHERE IT'S AT AND GAVE ME THE TOOLS
Yeah.

NOW I DON'T NEED A MAN TO TELL ME I COULD
STAY IN A CUSHY JOB THAT DON'T DO NO GOOD
SO I WILL TAKE A STAND CUZ I THINK I SHOULD
LIVE OUT A BIGGER PLAN LIKE MA SAID I WOULD

DO I KEEP A CAREER WITH THE STRESS UP TO HERE
JUST BECAUSE I MAKE SO MUCH GREEN?

No, I'll show some courage.
CUZ I'M MY OWN QUEEN!

I WILL NEVER SAY I CAN'T OR I NEED
THAT'S NOT A GAME I PLAY OR BOOK THAT I'LL READ
I'LL ALWAYS FIND A WAY TO WIN AND SUCCEED
BECAUSE EACH DAY'S A DAY FOR CHAINS TO BE FREED

SO I THRIVE AND SURVIVE ALL ALONE ON MY THRONE
WITH NO ONE BUT ME TO BE SEEN
IT'S HOW I WANT IT CUZ I'M MY OWN QUEEN!
I'M MY OWN, I'M MY OWN, I'M MY OWN QUEEN
I'M MY OWN, I'M MY OWN, I'M MY OWN QUEEN

MAMA ALWAYS TOLD ME TO BE TRUE TO YOUR SOUL
MAMA ALWAYS SHOWED ME THAT INNER STRENGTH DON'T
    GROW OLD
BLESS YOUR HEART DEAR MAMA, I HOPE YOU'RE LOOKING
    DOWN ON ME
AND YOU'RE PROUD THAT I'M LOUD ABOUT BEING
    ROYALTY? SEE

NO, NO MORE SLEEPLESS NIGHTS, AND HELL, NO MORE
    BLUES
MY FEAR IS OUT OF SIGHT SO HOW CAN I LOSE?
I'LL TAKE THE PATH TO LIGHT CUZ I GET TO CHOOSE
JUST HOW I LIVE MY LIFE CUZ I HEARD THE NEWS!!!!!
I'M MY OWN, I'M MY OWN, I'M MY OWN QUEEN
I'M MY OWN, I'M MY OWN, I'M MY OWN QUEEN

(She reaches under her desk, grabs a tiara and puts it on.)

MAMA, MAMA, MAMA I'M MY OWN QUEEN
I'M MY OWN, I'M MY OWN, I'M MY OWN QUEEN!!!

(She waves like Queen Elizabeth as lights fade.)

[MUSIC: No. 2A – "QUEEN PLAYOFF"]

Scene Three. The Elder Grille and Younger Boys Lounge

(MARY-MARIE is recording into her iPhone.)

MARY-MARIE. *'Life is perfect, whole and complete.'* Affirmation 7, *'My highest good now comes to pass as I trust the process of life.'* Number 8, *'I'm like a fine wine, I get better with age!'* That is good.

(She shuts off her device as BUCK enters.)

Oh, welcome, young man! Thank you so much for coming to interview at the Elder Grille and Younger Boys Lounge. Get it? 'Grille and Boys' – like 'Girl and Boy' but with a twist? I made the name up myself. It's like I channel it or something!

When I decided to build this here establishment, my financial advisor said to me, "Mary-Marie, you need to hire yourself a marketing company to help you brand your Cougar bar." But I said, "Oh Leo, now hush, cuz inside this Southern-fried woman is about ten Ben Franklin brains of brandin' genius." And the proof is in the sign. It says what it means and *that* is brandin' genius!

Well, Lordy me, I haven't introduced myself, now have I? I am Mary-Marie Beauregard de Cham*pain* – with an emphasis on the 'pain'. *(She slaps her ass.)* Well, that's enough about *me*. I got your resume right here but why don't cha tell me a little sumpin' sumpin' about *yourself?*

(On bell tone, lights change for male fantasy song. BUCK turns front and flashes a sparkling grin to audience and begins singing 'Swagger' while MARY-MARIE continues to read his resume, oblivious.)

[MUSIC: No. 3 – "SWAGGER"]

BUCK.
I AM THE HOT YOUNGER BUCK
WHO JUST RELIES ON HIS PLUCK

AND HIS LEGENDARY PHYSICAL ENDURANCE

I AM IN MY SEXUAL PRIME
WITH A BODY THE BEST IT'LL BE
THIS ADONIS STATE CAN LUBRICATE
ALMOST ANY GIRL THAT I SEE.
I DELIVER THE GOODS, NO IF'S, BUT'S OR SHOULD'S
THE LADIES RESPOND FAR AND NEAR
WITH MY APPETITE I CAN (UH!) ALL NITE
AND WHISPER SWEET THINGS IN HER EAR

I SWAGGER, YES, I SWAGGER,
WHEN I SWAGGER- IT MAKES ME FEEL STRONG
IF I SWAGGER THEN I CAN SHAG HER
CUZ THAT'S HOW DUDES HAVE DONE IT ALL ALONG

DON'T YOU THINK THAT I'M LOOKING GOOD?
MY BICEPS ARE SO OUT TO HERE
I CAN BENCH PRESS A CAR AND THEN THROW IT FAR

(back to reality)

MARY-MARIE. Can you also serve beer?

BUCK. Sure!

(back to fantasy)

GOT A SIX PACK AB AND THERE AIN'T NO FLAB
YOU KNOW I GOT SOMETHING TO SAY
SO I DO MY BEST TO PUFF UP MY CHEST
AND PHRASE IT LIKE YOUNG HEMINGWAY
SO I SWAGGER, YES I SWAGGER, WHEN I SWAGGER IT KEEPS
    ME ALIVE
IF I SWAGGER THEN I CAN SHAG HER
CAUSE THAT'S HOW DUDES HAVE DONE IT, THAT'S HOW
    DAD HAS DONE IT
THAT'S HOW WE WILL DO IT, THAT'S HOW WE'VE LEARNED
    TO SURVIVE!

MARY-MARIE. You're hired!!

(Blackout.)

Scene Four. The Park

(**LILY** *stands in front of a mailbox holding an envelope which contains her divorce papers. She starts to mail it and hesitates.*)

[MUSIC: No. 4 – "GARY'S RIGHT"]

LILY.

GARY WANTED DINNER AT FIVE FORTY FIVE,
HIS MARTINI DRY, HIS NEWS CHANNEL FIVE
GARY THOUGHT THE KIDS SHOULD BE SEEN AND NOT
    HEARD
SO I FED THEM FIRST AND DIDN'T SAY A WORD

Maybe if I'd just tried harder.

GARY WANTED WEEKENDS FOR SPORTS ON TV
HE COULDN'T CONCEIVE THAT I MIGHT BE FREE
GARY THOUGHT A WIFE SHOULD TAKE CARE OF THE HOME
SO I COOKED AND CLEANED THE HOUSE ON MY OWN.

I SHOULDN'T COMPLAIN, I MEAN IT'S PLAIN TO SEE
THAT GARY'S RIGHT. RIGHT?

WHEN GARY MET ME I WAS JUST THIRTY-TWO
I WAS WILLOWY THIN AND I DIDN'T HAVE A CLUE.
HE WAS SO DASHING, HE STOOD SIX FEET TALL
WITH BROAD SHOULDERS AND A FACE THAT MADE WOMEN
    FALL

Boy, did they ever...

GARY THOUGHT THE WEDDING SHOULD BE IN LATE MAY
SO I CANCELLED MY PLANS TO STAR IN MY FIRST PLAY.
I SHOULDN'T COMPLAIN, I MEAN WHERE WOULD I BE?
CUZ GARY'S RIGHT

YOU THINK THE HOUSE, THE CARS, THE JEWELS THAT
    THEY'D ALL SATISFY
THE FAINT, RUMBLING YEARNINGS OF ONE'S SOUL
AND THEN IT FINALLY HITS YOU THAT YOUR LIFE HAS
    PASSED YOU BY
NOW WHERE'S THE OTHER HALF

WHO'S SUPPOSED TO MAKE ME WHO-O-O-OLE?

(She paces.)

LA, LA, LA-LA-LA-LA
LA, LA, LA-LA-LA-LA
LA, LA, LA-LA-LA-LA
LA, LA, LA, LA!

GARY DIDN'T HOLD ME OR GAZE IN MY EYES,
HE WAS FULL OF EXCUSES AND FAKE ALIBIS
GARY WANTED ROMANCE - JUST NOT WITH ME.
HIS "SECRETARY" WORKED AFTER HOURS FOR FREE.

I MIGHT COMPLAIN BUT NOW I MUST AGREE
THAT GARY'S RIGHT, GARY'S RIGHT, GARY'S RIGHT
BUT HE'S NOT RIGHT FOR ME!

*(**LILY** courageously shoves the envelope into the mailbox. Blackout.)*

Scene Five. The Elder Grille and
Younger Boys Lounge

(MARY-MARIE sits at the bar, working on her computer.)

MARY-MARIE. Okey dokey, Smokey. Let me Google some more customers into my *den of antiquity*. Well, I've tried *Match.com, NoBaggage.com*, even *J-Date* and I'm a *shiksa*. But I do believe my synapses are flowing in the direction of...c'mon Google, search me baby, search me. Well, OK now! *CougarLife.com* – 'The world's largest and most trusted datin' site for women of a certain *demographic* and men of *another demographic* who have yet to *acquire* their baggage'.

(She begins to type, filling in her profile application.)

'Profile'...One: I am a woman. Two: 'Age'? Never ask a woman her age. Exclamation Point! Three: 'I am seeking a man in the age range of'? Mmmm...eighteen to twenty-five! No, too young. Nineteen to twenty-five. That's better. 'Profession': I own a Cougar Bar. 'Personal traits': I am into positive affirmations and I am so self loving that I am practically dating myself. So being with me will be like being in a threesome! R-r-r-r-r! If interested, contact Miss Kitty. *(She pushes 'Enter'.)* Submit!

(The bar phone rings.)

MARY-MARIE. Elder Grille Lounge, where the men are boys and the women are lucky. We are open from 4pm until delta dawn. Do we carry pomegranate juice and vanilla vodka? Let me check. *(She surveys the bar.)* Why, yes, yes, we do. OK, bye-bye now.

(LILY enters.)

LILY. Can I have a pomegranate juice and vanilla vodka?

MARY-MARIE. That was quick.

LILY. I was standing outside *(holds up her iPhone)* and I could not find POM juice anywhere. It's essential for my 'Over Forty' martini.

MARY-MARIE. What's this libation called?

LILY. I was thinking 'Drunken Divorce'.

MARY-MARIE. I'll come up with a name.

(holding out her hand)

I'm Mary-Marie. I don't believe I've seen your face in here before.

LILY. I've never been inside here before. I was doing *time*.

MARY-MARIE. Prison?

LILY. Marriage. But tonight is the first night of the rest of my life!

MARY-MARIE. Wow, my 'Affirmation #37' says the same darn thang. I am sensing some synergy here. What's your name?

LILY. Lily.

MARY-MARIE. Like the flower! Well, Lily, welcome to my Cougar bar.

(**MARY-MARIE** gestures for **LILY** to take a seat at the bar.)

LILY. Oh, that 'C' word. (She makes a sign of the cross with her fingers.) I read about this place in *New York Magazine*. But maybe it's too soon. Like I said, I just got divorced...*again*.

MARY-MARIE. Oh honey, I'm sorry.

LILY. Yeah, I married two guys named Gary. How is that possible?

MARY-MARIE. It's a common name. Gary, Indiana...

LILY. Gary #1: nice guy – father of my kids. Gary #2: Mr. Wonderful became Mr. Wonder-What-The-Fuck-Was-I-Thinking? Sorry, my 'singledom' is very new.

MARY-MARIE. How new?

LILY. Twenty-five minutes.

MARY-MARIE. Honey, this pomegranate and vodka is on me, and I'm gonna give it a name in your honor – 'Cougartini'. I can see the sign now. "Get your 'Cougartini' at the Elder Grille where the Younger Boys Lounge." It's exquisite marketin'.

(She hands her the Cougartini.)

LILY. Thanks. Listen, I'm not a whatever-you-call-it. I'm a mom. I bite my nails.

MARY-MARIE. No time like the present to see the light and get a manicure. I know the perfect place.

(Her cell phone rings. The ringtone is a Southern banjo riff a la The Beverly Hillbillies.)

Excuse me. *(She answers the phone.)* Oh Frank, it's you again. Can't talk now, I'm in a business meetin'. Tuesday? I think my hair will be dryin'. Sorry. *(She hangs up.)* This man keeps calling to ask me out but he's way too old so I say no on principle.

LILY. How old?

MARY-MARIE. Fifty-four.

LILY. And you are?

MARY-MARIE. Fifty-four. Honey, I will never be with a man my age ever again. Been there, done that, thanks to my dearly departed Henry- may he rest in pieces.

LILY. Oh, I'm so sorry.

MARY-MARIE. Don't get me wrong, he was a real peach. Just no Prince Charmin' in the bedroom. His idea of foreplay was watchin' the first half hour of Bill Maher on HBO.

LILY. Oh, no.

MARY-MARIE. No matter. I may not have known passion but I was sure up on my current events. Anyway, if life is craps then the dice I'm now throwin' are younger men.

LILY. Father-figure issues. I like older men.

MARY-MARIE. Come on, honey, who can forget Cher and the Bagel Boy? I bet there was more than dough risin'! Besides, you are drinking a Cougartini at a Cougar bar…

LILY. So?

MARY-MARIE. So be present to the opportunity. Look over there at five o'clock.

LILY. Who? The boy in the *Twilight* tee shirt? He's my daughters' age.

MARY-MARIE. Tap that boy's ass in honor of your new life!

LILY. What? You mean objectify him as a sexual object? God, that sounds so…

MARY-MARIE. Good?

LILY. No. It sounds like…

MARY-MARIE. Fun?

LILY. No. It sounds like an empty sexual act devoid of any real personal connection. God, Mary-Marie, come on, that sounds like…

MARY-MARIE. Like…

LILY. Like…a guy!

[MUSIC: No. 4A – "TWILIGHT CROSS"]

(A young man in a Twilight t-shirt saunters over. Twilight Zone theme)

MARY-MARIE. Well, hello there, young man. I like the t-shirt. Team Jacob or Edward?

TWILIGHT DUDE. Oh, I'm into *The Hunger Games* now. Mind if I join you?

LILY. Are you serious? *(to* **MARY-MARIE***)* Is he on your payroll?

*(***MARY-MARIE*** winks and exits.)*

Excuse me, are you for real?

TWILIGHT DUDE. What's your definition of real?

LILY. Not sure. My definition seems to be evolving. Or these drinks are laced with peyote and I'm hallucinating! Kidding. Last time I did peyote I was at a Bob Seger concert.

TWILIGHT DUDE. Who's Bob Seger?

LILY. Ah, you seem like a very young, I mean, very nice, young man.

TWILIGHT DUDE. And you seem a little on edge. How about a back rub? Let me massage those troubles away?

LILY. Right here? Right now?

TWILIGHT DUDE. Sure.

LILY. I don't think so.

(He starts to rub her shoulders.)

Oh, God, that feels good! I really have been stressed lately. If you must know I just got divorced and now that I'm newly single I feel like I have the weight of the WORLD on my shoulders.

TWILIGHT DUDE. Is that too hard?

LILY. No, I like it hard. I mean, I like it deep. I mean Holy Mother of God, where have you been the last ten years of my life?

TWILIGHT DUDE. High school?

[MUSIC: No. 5 – "THE COUGAR"]

LILY.

IF THURSDAY'S THE NEW FRIDAY
AND PINK IS THE NEW BLACK?
THEN FORTY'S THE NEW THIRTY, SO TIME IS TURNING BACK
THERE'S A MOVEMENT COMING, I SAW IT ON TV
GOT ITS' NAME FROM THE FAME OF

TWILIGHT DUDE.

ASHTON AND DEMI

LILY. *(spoken emphatically)* But before they broke up and she went into rehab.

TWILIGHT DUDE. That is so two years ago.

LILY.

INSIDE THIS PERI-MENOPAUSAL BODY I DO FIND

TWILIGHT DUDE.

A VERY SEXY HOTTIE WHO'S JUST WAITING TO UNWIND

LILY.

I'VE HAD MY KIDS AND HUSBANDS, TOO
MY BAGGAGE HAS BEEN PLENTY

TWILIGHT DUDE.

AND NOW THE MEN WHO HIT ON YOU
ARE SOMEWHERE AROUND TWENTY
YOU'LL BE TURNING HEADS IN DESIGNER THREADS

LILY.

> EAT STEAK AT PETER LUGER
>
> AND MY DATING POOL JUST GOT OUT OF SCHOOL, NO WAY!

TWILIGHT DUDE. Yeah, you're a cougar!

LILY. *(insulted)* Cougar? And what do you call an older man who dates a younger woman? I've researched it. It's called MAN!

TWILIGHT DUDE.

> A COUGAR IS A WOMAN, EMPOWERED, STRONG WITH LOOT
>
> SHE LOOKS FINE WHILE SIPPING WINE IN HER ARMANI SUIT
>
> SHE'S LIVED ENOUGH TO HAVE GROWN WISE
>
> BUT LOOK INTO HER BEDROOM EYES

LILY.

> WHO KNEW THAT BOYS WOULD FANTASIZE

TWILIGHT DUDE.

> AND OLDER GALS COULD TANTALIZE?
>
> WHAT MATTERS IS A ZEST FOR LIFE. A BRAIN, A WIT.

LILY.

> AND FASHION

TWILIGHT DUDE.

> AND COUGAR'S THE NEW NAME FOR IT

LILY.

> AND YOU CAN BE MY PASSION!

(He leads her in a crazy salsa.)

TWILIGHT DUDE.

> LET'S BLOW THIS SCENE AND DO THE TOWN –I'LL TAKE
>
>> YOU OUT, MY DEAR
>
> AS LONG AS YOU ARE SATISFIED WITH FAST FOOD AND
>
>> CHEAP BEER

*(**LILY** reacts.)*

> IF YOU COME BACK TO MY PLACE, I'LL PULL OUT
>
>> MY GUITAR

LILY.

> BUT THIS OLD BROAD'S GOT STANDARDS SO YOU MIGHT
>
>> NOT GET TOO FAR.
>
> INSIDE I FEEL I'M THIRTY-TWO

TWILIGHT DUDE.

OUTSIDE YOU'RE LOOKING THIRTY

LILY.

YOU SAY THE SWEETEST THINGS, YOUNG MAN,

I CAN'T HELP BUT GET ALL FLIRTY

AND NOW I KNOW I'M NOT ALONE, THERE'S OTHERS JUST
LIKE ME

J-LO AND HER DANCER BOY, ASHTON AND DEMI

TWILIGHT DUDE. But before they broke up

LILY.

I'M HAVING FUN LIKE I'M TWENTY ONE

MY LOVE IS SWEET AS S-U-GAR

TWILIGHT DUDE AND LILY.

AND MY/HER DATING POOL JUST GOT OUT OF SCHOOL,
OK!

TWILIGHT DUDE. I'm hot for COUGAR!

*(In musical interlude, **LILY** 'fluffs' up her breasts and checks her breath and **TWILIGHT DUDE** slicks back his hair.)*

WHAT ARE YOUR PLANS NEXT THURSDAY NIGHT?

LILY.

CAUSE THURSDAY'S THE NEW FRIDAY

TWILIGHT DUDE.

LET'S PAINT THE TOWN AND TRIP THE LIGHT

LILY.

WE'LL HAVE SOME FUN BUT MY WAY

*(**TWILIGHT DUDE** 'dips' her and looks more closely at her face.)*

TWILIGHT DUDE. *(sincerely)*

HEY, YOU KNOW, I'VE GOTTA SAY

THAT YOU REMIND ME OF ANOTHER

CLASSY, CHIC AND FINE LADY

YOU LOOK JUST LIKE MY MOTHER.

*(**LILY** is crushed.)*

TWILIGHT DUDE. *(looking at his watch)* O jeez. Well, gotta dash, watch the last half of NASCAR and get ready for my SATs.

(He walks away, turns back and looks at **LILY**.*)*

You do. You look just like my mom!

(He exits. **MARY-MARIE** *enters.)*

LILY. Don't you check IDs?!

MARY-MARIE. Of course I do. He's legal just educationally challenged. Besides…

(Music resumes.)

MARY-MARIE.
>WHAT MATTERS IS A ZEST FOR LIFE, A BRAIN, A WIT AND PASSION
>AND YOU ARE GONNA GO FOR IT IN FULL TILT COUGAR FASHION!
>YOU'LL BE TURNING HEADS IN DESIGNER THREADS

LILY.
>MY LOVE IS SWEET AS SUGAR

MARY-MARIE.
>AND OUR DATING POOL JUST GOT OUT OF SCHOOL, OK!

LILY.
>NO WAY!

MARY-MARIE.
>YOU ARE

LILY.
>I'M NOT

BOTH.
>A COUGAR!

*(***MARY-MARIE*** is joyous.* **LILY** *is skeptical. Blackout.)*

[MUSIC: No. 5A – "THE COUGAR PLAYOFF"]

Scene Six. Outside 'Eve's Nail Salon'/ Inside 'Eve's Nail Salon'

(As CLARITY *approaches, her cell phone rings. She answers.)*

CLARITY. Oh, Martin, I'm so glad you called! Your mother left the bank. Yes, I decided to go for it, son. Now I'll be able to teach women's studies. Can you believe it? Professor Jackson! Only now I am stressing about using my mind fulltime for study, I've got to write my prospectus by Monday and my brain is a sieve. Martin, I'm kinda embarrassed to ask but any advice to help your mama focus? ...Amphetamines, Red Bull and Adderall? Good thing my son is a pharmacist! Alright, darling, I've got to run. Wish me luck.

*(*CLARITY *enters Eve's Nail Salon to the sound of Asian wind chimes.)*

EVE. Oh Clarity, so nice to see you! *(a la Wendy Williams)* How you doin'?

CLARITY. Hi, Eve! Oh, I am in a horrible state.

EVE. New Jersey?

CLARITY. No, I am just stressed. Change is stressful. I just met with my graduate advisor to pitch my thesis.

EVE. What you write about?

*(*EVE *prepares her manicure station.)*

CLARITY. I've decided to expound on the 'Cougar' phenomenon. I will set out to prove that it is a derogatory term, perpetuating the self-loathing of the modern female after a millennium of patriarchal dictation!

EVE. Well, nothing that a 'mani-pedi' can't cure! Please make yourself at home while I go find your color, 'Regal Red'.

CLARITY. Thanks, Eve.

*(*EVE *exits as* CLARITY *opens a large, hardbound book.* MARY-MARIE *enters in her Cougar regalia, staring at her iPhone.)*

MARY-MARIE. OOOHWEE! Two more replies in my inbox. One from Bourbon Cowboy and another from a young man named Goliath who says he will 'slay me'.

*(She sees **CLARITY**.)*

Oh, I didn't see you behind that big book. I'm Mary-Marie.

CLARITY. Clarity Jackson.

MARY-MARIE. Do you often hide behind big books?

CLARITY. *(polite yet distracted)* Oh, this? I'm researching my thesis for grad school.

MARY-MARIE. School?

CLARITY. I just left a major job as a financial analyst.

MARY-MARIE. See there, we already have something in common because you worked in finance and I'm steeped in finances.

CLARITY. Well, bills do need to be paid.

MARY-MARIE. Yessiree! Bills and Dicks and Harrys, I pay them all! Good thing I'm independently wealthy.

CLARITY. Too bad I didn't know you back in the day.

MARY-MARIE. Well, I am pretty much a 'Jacqueline' of all trades – a Renaissance Woman. And I own a brand new Cougar bar.

CLARITY. *(perking up)* A Cougar bar? Really?

MARY-MARIE. Oh, yeah. I am giving birth to new ideas all the time. I am working on an app for the iPhone which will be entitled, "Affirmations For The Woman Over Forty". I just thought of one on my way over here, "It's never too late to teach an old dog new tricks...you just need a really big bone." That's good. Isn't that good?

CLARITY. Yes, very astute. But I would like to talk to you about your Cougar bar.

*(**EVE** enters carrying two bottles of nail polish.)*

EVE. Oh, Mary-Marie! *(a la Wendy Williams)* How you doin'? I have your color right here. *(She holds the bottle further away to read better.)* 'Some Young Flesh'?

*(**EVE** puts the bottle on **MARY-MARIE**'s table.)*

MARY-MARIE. Say, Eve, I invited my new friend to get her nails done. She's coming right from work and I don't think she has ever had a manicure.

CLARITY/EVE. *(gasping)* What!!!

MARY MARIE. It's tragic.

EVE. I change her life! **(EVE** *sits down to manicure* **CLARITY**'s *nails. Vamp begins.)* Clarity…let me see your paw. *(a la Wendy Williams)* How you doin?

[MUSIC: No. 6 – "SHINY AND NEW"]

CLARITY.

I DO BELIEVE IN THE GOOD THAT WILL BE
BUT I AM NOT USED TO THIS ANXIETY
I SUPPOSE THAT THIS NEXT YEAR OF CLASSROOMS AND
    WRITING
WILL BECOME A CAREER THAT IS FUN AND EXCITING.

So Eve.

MAKE ME FEEL GOOD LIKE THE FIRST TIME
SHINY AND NEW LIKE THE FIRST TIME
GIVE ME THE NAILS TO HELP ME GET UP THE NERVE
AND FIND THE HAPPINESS THAT I DESERVE!

(EVE *maneuvers her rolling stool to* **MARY-MARIE**'s *manicure station.)*

MARY-MARIE. I know what you mean. I'm in new territory myself.

MY INBOX SAID I'VE GOT FOURTEEN REPLIES
FROM ALL SORTS OF FABULOUS NINETEEN YEAR OLD GUYS
MY ONLY DILEMNA IS STACKING THE MEETINGS
SO EACH BOY WILL ENJOY A MIRACULOUS GREETING!

So Eve.

MAKE ME FEEL STRONG LIKE THE FIRST TIME
POINTY AND LONG LIKE THE FIRST TIME
GIVE ME THE NAILS TO HELP ME GET UP MY NERVE
TO FIND THE ORGASM THAT I DESERVE!

(Vamp continues as **LILY** *walks in dressed in her 'Dorothy' outfit.)*

EVE. Welcome to Eve's! You look like you are from Wizard of Oz!

LILY. Sorry I'm late.

*(***EVE** *grabs* **LILY***'s hand in horror, and throws her toward the manicure station.)*

EVE. Ooh, looks like Toto chew on your CUTICLE!

LILY. OH! *(She sits.)* Mary-Marie, please forgive me. My party went overtime. I had to paint rainbows on thirty six-year-old kids' faces!

MARY-MARIE. Thirty-six-year-old kids? What was it? A brothel?

LILY. No. Six-year-old kids. Thirty of 'em. Couldn't click my heels fast enough.

*(***EVE** *sits on stool and begins* **LILY***'s nails.)*

MY LIFE HAS GONE FROM CRASHING TO BURN
I'M SURE THERE IS SOME LARGER LESSON TO LEARN
I FEEL SO ALONE WITHOUT A GUY THERE BESIDE ME
I'M OUT OF MY ZONE WHEN THERE'S NO ONE TO GUIDE ME.

So Eve.

MAKE ME FEEL GOOD, IT'S MY FIRST TIME
SHE SAID THAT YOU WOULD, IT'S MY FIRST TIME
GIVE ME THE NAILS TO HELP ME GET UP THE NERVE
AND FIND THE SELF ESTEEM THAT I DESERVE

MARY-MARIE.

I TRIED THE RED FOR LOVE
THEN MESSED IT WITH MY GLOVE

CLARITY.

THOUGHT SILVER WOULD BE GRAND
DIDN'T LOOK GOOD ON MY HAND

MARY-MARIE.

WENT FRENCH THEN BROKE A TIP

EVE.

OH, THAT WOULD MAKE ME FLIP!

ALL THREE.

> IT'S NO SURPRISE THAT THEN
> WE NEED TO RETURN HERE AGAIN
> AND AGAIN AND AGAIN!

EVE.

> 2-3-4!

> *(Music pulls back as* **EVE** *leads a kick line a la The Rockettes.)*

ALL THREE.

> MAKE ME FEEL GOOD LIKE THE FIRST TIME
> SHINY AND NEW LIKE THE FIRST TIME
> GIVE ME THE NAILS TO HELP ME GET UP THE NERVE
> AND FIND THE HAPPINESS THAT I DE –

> MAKE ME FEEL BOLD LIKE THE FIRST TIME

EVE.

> AAAAH!!!

ALL THREE.

> YOUNG BUT NOT OLD LIKE THE FIRST TIME

EVE.

> AAAAH!!!

ALL THREE.

> GIVE ME THE NAILS, I'LL SCRATCH YOUR BACK, YOU
>   SCRATCH MINE
> AND FIND OUR HAPPINESS AND MAKE IT SHINE,
> MAKE IT SHINE, MAKE IT SHINE,

EVE.

> AAHH! AAHH!

ALL THREE.

> MAKE IT SHINE, MAKE IT...

EVE. Oh, be careful of the nails!

ALL THREE PLUS EVE.

> SHINE!

> *(Blackout.)*

[MUSIC: No. 6A – "SHINY AND NEW PLAYOFF"]

Scene Seven. Mary-Marie's Office/"Boudoir".

(MARY-MARIE enters in a fringed cowboy jacket. Her cell phone rings.)

MARY-MARIE. Frank? No, this isn't a good time. I'm preparing for a business meetin'. *(She hisses a sound into the phone, imitating static.)* Can you hear me now? *(She hisses more static.)* How about now? Darn, I lost ya.

(BOURBON COWBOY enters in jeans, boots and a cowboy hat.)

BOURBON COWBOY. *(with a Texas drawl)* Yoo hoo!

MARY MARIE. Well, howdy partner!

BOURBON COWBOY. Well, howdy Ma'am! I'm the Bourbon Cowboy.

MARY-MARIE. Welcome to my corral!

BOURBON COWBOY. Thank you.

MARY-MARIE. I dare say I reckon to give you a what-for!

BOURBON COWBOY. And then a what-five and what-six?

MARY-MARIE. And a what-seven! Yee-haw!

(MARY-MARIE and BOURBON COWBOY are in two separate spots and they never touch but simulate touching. She smacks his ass like she's riding a bronco.)

Giddy up now, Pony Boy, show me your horse power!

BOURBON COWBOY. You sure ain't one fer small talk!

MARY-MARIE. Hell, small talk's fer when you can't think big. What do you say I school you in the wily ways of the west? Lemme lasso that libido!

BOURBON COWBOY. Whoa there, filly!

MARY-MARIE. Filly? That'd be a 'mare'. In fact, a 'Mare-y-Marie' which means I do twice the matin'!

BOURBON COWBOY. I'm not quite sure I'm comfortable with this…

MARY-MARIE. Let's try another position then. Doggy-style! Ooooheeee!

(**BOURBON COWBOY** *pulls himself away from her.*)

BOURBON COWBOY. Excuse me! I know I showed up here wearing chaps and all but that doesn't mean that I signed on for this sort of thang. Can I have my hat back?

(**MARY-MARIE** *picks up the hat.*)

MARY-MARIE. Well, you said in your profile that you were into role playin' so I thought...

BOURBON COWBOY. I just thought I'd come and have some fun conversation and possible...

(*He indicates the chaise lounge.*)

...you know. But you are –

(*He begins to choke up.*)

– whoa, coming on way too strong...I'm not cheap!

(*He grabs his hat and exits.*)

(*Musical sting*)

[MUSIC: No. 6B – "LILY'S CROSSOVER"]

MARY-MARIE. Dang!

(*Blackout*)

(*Transition to Street, "Shiny and New" underscore*)

(**LILY** *crosses with a Bloomingdale's bag. She pauses, pulls out a new Cougar dress and holds it up, looking at her reflection in a store window. She likes what she sees, puts the dress back in the bag and exits.*)

Scene Eight. Elder Grille and Younger Boys Lounge

(**MARY-MARIE** *is looking glum and sipping a high ball. She records into her iPhone.*)

MARY-MARIE. 'There are no bad experiences only experiences'. *(She puts her head down on the bar.)* Dang.

(**BUCK** *enters.*)

BUCK. Mary-Marie, what are you drinking?

MARY-MARIE. *(without lifting her head)* Bourbon and Shame.

BUCK. You look pale. Can I get you anything? A seltzer? A pillow?

MARY-MARIE. You are a nice boy, Buck, so handsome and kind. I bet you've always been a real ladies man.

BUCK. Nah, actually I was a kind of shy type. Straight A's, into my sports. In college I dated this girl, Lorna.

MARY-MARIE. Like the cookie, Lorna Doone?

BUCK. Yeah. We were pretty serious but after we graduated, she decided to go back to Ohio and I stayed in New York to become a Broadway star and I am currently... the best bartender in Manhattan!

MARY-MARIE. You seem real smart.

BUCK. Gee, thanks. Well, my dad wanted me to join his law firm and I aced the LSATs and got into two great law schools. But it wasn't for me.

(**LILY** *walks in wearing her new dress.*)

MARY-MARIE. Hey Lily, over here! Nice dress!

LILY. Thanks.

MARY-MARIE. Buck, what do you say you open up a nice bottle of Chardonnay? Cuz I feel like whinin'.

(**BUCK** *checks* **LILY** *out and then exits to get the wine.*)

LILY. You OK?

MARY-MARIE. Let's just say my Western Consort was no Southern Comfort!

LILY. That's too bad.

MARY-MARIE. Yeah, well, I'm gittin' right back on the ole horse but that's enough about me.

(CLARITY walks into the bar.)

MARY-MARIE. Clarity, welcome! Come on in.

CLARITY. *(looking around)* Wow! Mary Marie, this is really something!

LILY. *(flaunting her new nails)* Hey…

CLARITY. Nice nails.

MARY MARIE. Come over here and have a seat. Let me fix you a Cougartini. Tell Lily what it is you do!

(CLARITY opens her mouth to speak but MARY-MARIE interrupts.)

This lady is a brilliant sociopolitical writer who reads big books for her…?

CLARITY. Masters in Women's Studies.

LILY. Women's Studies?

MARY-MARIE. I told her about my Affirmation app and she wants to follow us around and gather important information. Isn't that right, Clarity?

LILY. Ah, "clarity". I sure could use some of that right now.

CLARITY. Why? What's the problem? You ladies mind if I start taking notes?

LILY. No. Maybe you can figure out why I feel so lost when I'm alone. When I was two, my dad took me to a department store. First time away from the mother ship. It was raining and he instructed me to hang onto the bottom of his rain coat.

CLARITY. Why didn't he hold your hand?

LILY. Not his style.

MARY-MARIE. You were only two!

LILY. Yeah well, that was so forty-five years ago. Anyway, Burberry must have been the rage because somehow I latched onto another man's raincoat.

CLARITY. Whoa.

LILY. It's a metaphor for my life. I'm still looking for that hand to hold.

CLARITY. Oh Lily, you don't need a man. My mother raised four kids on her own and never looked back. I raised my boy, Martin, alone. Sure, I wanted love and affection, but I couldn't have a man in my bed with him sleeping in the next room. So I got used to my own company. And you can too.

LILY. No, I can't. I panic when I'm alone.

CLARITY. Lily, you don't need a king to be a queen.

[MUSIC: No. 7 – "SAY YES"]

CLARITY.

WHEN YOU THINK YOUR LIFE'S A MESS, SAY YES!
WHEN YOU CAN'T ZIP UP YOUR FAVORITE DRESS, SAY YES!
SAY YES TO THE MAN WHO DUMPED YOU
HE'S A JERK, SO WHAT, MOVE ON
JUST WATCH, 'CAUSE WHEN THE WIND STARTS TO BLOW

LILY.

I'LL SAY NO

CLARITY.

NO, YOU'LL SAY YES!

MARY-MARIE.

WHEN YOU'VE LOST YOUR QUEEN IN CHESS, SAY YES!
WHEN YOUR BOAT IS IN DISTRESS, SAY YES!
SAY YES TO THE ROAD LESS TRAVELED
IT'S ROCKY, WHO KNEW, BIG DEAL

LILY.

SO I'LL FIND MYSELF ANOTHER WAY TO GO, OH NO

CLARITY/MARY-MARIE.

OH YES!
WHEN YOU FEEL LIKE THERE IS NO MORE HOPE

CLARITY.

DON'T MOPE, MY FRIEND

MARY-MARIE.

DON'T YOU MOPE

CLARITY.

WHEN YOU SHOWER

CLARITY/MARY-MARIE.

AND THERE AIN'T NO SOAP?

CLARITY.

YOU'LL COPE

LILY.

I'LL COPE

CLARITY/MARY-MARIE.

DON'T COMPLAIN IF YOUR TEAM LOSES

LILY.

LIFE GIVES US SOME BRUISES

ALL THREE.

THAT'S THE WAY IT SEEMS TO BE

SOMETIMES THERE'S NO POETRY

MARY-MARIE.

WHEN YOU FEEL SMALL IN THE CHEST

LILY. Hey!

MARY-MARIE. Oh please. SAY YES

LILY.

WHEN THE NORTHERN STAR STAYS IN THE WEST…SAY YES?

CLARITY/MARY-MARIE.

YES!

ALL THREE.

WHEN YOU WANNA CRY LIKE A BABY

DRESS UP LIKE A LADY

LILY.

THE GAME OF LIFE CAN BE A TEST

CLARITY.

BUT HANG IN THERE, YOU'LL SOON BE BLESSED

(Song changes to gospel feel)

LILY.

IF I JUST SAY YES?

CLARITY/MARY-MARIE.

YES, YES, YEH-E-EH-E-EH-S, YES

LILY.

IF I JUST SAY YES

CLARITY/MARY-MARIE.

YES, YES, YES, YEH-E-EH-E-S!

LILY.

IF I JUST SAY YES TO THE LOSS, YES TO THE PAIN
YES TO THE MESS AND THE STRESS AND THE STRAIN

CLARITY/MARY-MARIE.

DON'T GIVE UP MY FRIEND, JUST FIGHT TO THE END
A BETTER DAY'S COMIN' IF YOU JUST SAY YES

LILY.

I AM A WOMAN, HEAR ME ROAR

CLARITY/MARY-MARIE.

IF I JUST SAY YES

LILY.

IN SUCH NUMBERS YOU CAN'T IGNORE

CLARITY/MARY-MARIE.

IF I JUST SAY YES

LILY.

ALL I GOTTA DO IS CELEBRATE

CLARITY/MARY-MARIE.

(simultaneously singing with **LILY***)*

OOH, OOH, OOH-OOH-OOH-OOH, OOH, CELEBRATE!

ALL THREE.

FOR MY HIGHEST GOOD IS ON ITS WAY
IF I JUST SAY YES

MARY-MARIE.

YES

CLARITY.

YES

LILY.

YES

ALL THREE.

SAY YES!
IF I JUST SAY YES

MARY-MARIE.

YES

CLARITY.

YES

LILY.
> YEH- EH- ES! SAY YES

CLARITY/MARY-MARIE.
> OOH-OOH-OOH

ALL THREE.
> YES!

> *(The three women strike a unified pose raising their arms in exultation.)*

MARY-MARIE. Come on, Clarity, I want to show you my boudoir.

CLARITY. Oh, you've got a boudoir!

> *(CLARITY and MARY-MARIE exit as LILY turns away from the bar and continues to groove on "Say Yes" song. Unseen, BUCK enters and watches her.)*

BUCK. Hello there.

LILY. *(startled)* Hi.

BUCK. I'm Buck.

LILY. I'm Lily. Are you new?

BUCK. No, I've been around 24 years. The Grille, a couple of weeks. That's a lifetime in Mary-Marie years.

LILY. Yeah. She's a real pip.

BUCK. She sure is.

> *(BUCK wipes down the counter and puts up bar stools.)*

LILY. You look familiar. I don't know, what do you do when you're not tending bar?

BUCK. I'm an actor.

LILY. Oh nice! I almost got to do that but life got in the way. What's it like?

BUCK. Well, I'm a straight guy in musical theatre. Kind of an oxymoron.

LILY. Like a skinny chef.

BUCK. Bah-du-bum!

> *(LILY imitates a cymbal hit.)*

BUCK. No, I just wish I were working more. I mean, I graduated NYU Drama and I thought if I knew how to dance and act and sing, I'd be all set. But nowadays, you gotta play an instrument while roller skating and blowing bubbles.

LILY. The closest I've come to performing is warbling show tunes to six year-olds.

BUCK. You're a warbler?

LILY. Oh, God, this is gonna come back and haunt me, isn't it?

BUCK. Well, I do like the 'come back' part.

(He crosses to turn off the bar lights.)

LILY. Wow. Hey, if you could do anything you could ever want without fear of failure, what would it be?

BUCK. Whoa! Total non-sequitor! Seriously?

LILY. Seriously. You can have, do or be anything you want.

BUCK. God, I don't know. I never think about that.

LILY. Maybe you should start.

BUCK. Maybe I will. *(He puts on his jacket.)* How 'bout you?

LILY. What?

BUCK. What would Lily do if she had no fear of failure?

LILY. God, I don't know. I really don't like talking about myself.

*(**BUCK** hands **LILY** her purse.)*

BUCK. Aw, come on, tell me about the *real* you.

LILY. Okay…

(During the song, they take a walk through the park.)

[MUSIC: No. 8 – "LET'S TALK ABOUT ME"}

LILY. *(grasping for straws)*
DEEPAK CHOPRA IS SO WISE
AND GEORGE CLOONEY HAS NICE EYES
MANOLO BLAHNIK, HE DESIGNED A REAL NICE SHOE

BUCK. Okay…

LILY.

> STEPHEN HAWKING'S KINDA SMART
> AND PICASSO COULD DO ART

BUCK.

> BUT ENOUGH OF THEM
> LET'S TALK ABOUT YOU

LILY. *(more confident)*

> ALVIN AILEY HAD THE BEAT
> FELIX UNGER WAS REAL NEAT
> EVA GABOR ENJOYED A PENTHOUSE VIEW
> MARGERET SANGER FOUGHT FOR RIGHTS
> NUREYEV LOOKED GOOD IN TIGHTS

BUCK.

> BUT ENOUGH OF THEM LET'S TALK ABOUT YOU
> I CAN'T HELP BUT FIND YOUR HISTORY ENTHRALLING
> THE WHO, WHAT, WHERE AND HOW OF YOU

LILY.

> SNOW, RAIN AND SUN AND WHEN THE LEAVES ARE FALLING
> I STILL HAVEN'T GIVEN YOU A CLUE

BUCK.

> GENERAL CUSTER HAD A STAND

LILY.

> PAUL MCCARTNEY HAD A BAND

BUCK.

> DIAN FOSSEY STUDIED MONKEYS

LILY. No, it was apes.

BUCK.

> IN A TREE
> I loved that movie.

LILY. Me, too!

BUCK.

> MR. GHANDI HAD A CAUSE

LILY.

> AND SO DOES SANTA CLAUS

BUCK. Ho-ho-ho.

LILY. I know,

    LET'S TALK ABOUT ME

BUCK. Well?

LILY. So, I'm into biking and hiking…

BUCK. Yeah, and "long walks on the beach". Very funny.

LILY.

    GEORGE HAMILTON HAS A TAN

BUCK.

    OBAMA HAD A PLAN

LILY. Has.

BUCK.

    SAM ADAMS MAKES A FINE AND HEARTY BREW

LILY.

    CLEOPATRA RULED THE NILE AND RALPH LAUREN HAS
        SOME STYLE

BUCK.

    BUT ENOUGH OF THEM, LET'S TALK ABOUT YOU

LILY.

    CRAIG FERGUSON HAS A GOOD SHOW

BUCK.

    KEITH RICHARDS SNORTED BLOW

BOTH.

    'SLUMDOG' WON…

    (They pause, realizing they are thinking the same thing.)

    THE OSCAR TROPHY

LILY. I loved that movie.

BUCK. Danny Boyle rocks!

LILY.

    I'M OVER FORTY-FIVE

BUCK.

    AND I'M OLD ENOUGH… TO DRIVE

BOTH.

    BUT ENOUGH OF THEM, LET'S TALK ABOUT

LILY.

    ME!

(She takes out a pen, writes her phone number on his hand and gestures "Call me." Fade to black as they part ways.)

[MUSIC: No. 8A – "LET'S TALK ABOUT ME PLAYOFF"}

Scene Nine. Mary-Marie's Office/"Boudoir"

(CLARITY *is reading a People Magazine.* MARY-MARIE *is exercising vigorously.*)

MARY-MARIE. So I said boxers or briefs? And he said, "I go *commando!*" So I commanded him to briefly drop his drawers and I pretended I was a boxer. It was an amazing experience of sex, fun, and alliteration.

CLARITY. Did you know that Madonna is dating a Spanish boy-toy thirty years her junior?

MARY-MARIE. Oh honey, that old rag is so two years ago. I just keep it for easy readin' on the loo.

CLARITY. Well, it says here: "MADONNA LEADS JESUS INTO KABALA"... I find that ironic.

(*She picks up notebook and pen.*)

Speaking of irony, how does your son feel about your lifestyle?

MARY-MARIE. Henry Junior? We don't chat about my lifestyle on Facebook or nothin'. He has a trust fund and I trust that he's havin' fun! See what I mean about alliteration?

CLARITY. Does he know that you are a serial Cougar?

MARY-MARIE. You make it sound like an affliction or unlawful!

CLARITY. Well if "forty's the new thirty", then "twenty is the new ten"... and isn't that illegal?

MARY-MARIE. If they are over eighteen, they can have my 'cereal' for breakfast anytime.

(MARY-MARIE *starts to gyrate vigorously.*)

CLARITY. What are you doing?

MARY-MARIE. My dance to The Sacred Feminine. And as for my son, he is a grown man. Right now, we're taking a temporary sabbatical. We haven't spoken for the last six months, per his request, so he could go 'find himself'. But I know he wants his mama to be happy and self expressed. I'm sure your Martin wants that for you!

CLARITY. Oh trust me, I am self expressed. I do what I want, when I want.

MARY-MARIE. Uh huh…

CLARITY. I just don't want a younger man. No substance.

MARY-MARIE. Clarity, after Henry Senior died, I gave myself the space to live in grace. I know I rhymed but I'm making a point. I am now in the missionary position to make a difference in these boys' lives. Like a good will ambassador.

CLARITY. Good for you, Mary-Marie…I think. But if there were a grown up out there who could fill my needs and not talk back, I'd marry him. Anyway, I already have the sex partner of my dreams.

MARY-MARIE. Really? Do tell.

[MUSIC: No. 9 – "JULIO"]

CLARITY.

I HAVE GOT A FRIEND IN MY LIFE
AND I KEEP HIM CLOSE TO ME
I WISH THAT I COULD INTRODUCE HIM
HE IS CALLED JULIO

WHENEVER I AM IN SOME TROUBLE
AND I NEED A HELPING HAND *(SOMETIMES I DO)*
I KNOW THAT I CAN RELY ON
MY FRIEND JULIO

WHENEVER I AM LONELY
HE'S THE ONE AND ONLY
I NEED TO CALL
HE'S NEVER IN A HURRY
I DON'T HAVE TO WORRY
HE'S GONNA GIVE IT HIS ALL

(With each "AHHH", CLARITY pulses and reaches an orgasmic state.)

AHH- AHH- AHH- AHH- AHH- AHH- AHHHHHHHH!

(She breaks into giggles.)

Oh, Julio! You naughty, little thing.

I call you...PLASTIC MAN!

I HAVE GOT A PAL IN MY LIFE
CONSIDERATE AND HANDSOME TOO
HE'S REALLY VERY ENTERTAINING
MY DEAR JULIO

WHENEVER I AM FEELING TRAGIC
HE WHISTLES ME A HAPPY TUNE, Z-Z-Z-Z!
IT'S WONDERFUL HE DOESN'T TALK MUCH
MY SWEET JULIO

IF I NEED ATTENTION
I JUST HAVE TO MENTION
A RENDEZVOUS
HE'S HAPPY TO OBLIGE ME
LYING HERE BESIDE ME
HE LOVES TO PLAY PEEK-A-BOO!

Ooh!

AHH- AHH- AHH- AHH- AHH- AHH-
    AHHHHHHHHHHHHHHHHHHHH!

Sometimes you just gotta hand it to technology!

(**MARY-MARIE** and **CLARITY** *share a hoot while exiting.*)

[MUSIC: No. 9A – "JULIO PLAYOFF"]

Scene Ten. Church Basement, Room F

(LILY runs in excitedly, wearing a raincoat as well as cat ears on her head.)

LILY. Hello, my 'Over Forty and Fabulous' sisters! How the hell are you? Sorry I'm late but I had to do a Catwoman for a bunch of thirteen-year-old boys at a birthday party in the Village. And with these nails, I couldn't peel off the suit.

(She opens her coat and flashes her sexy Catwoman outfit. She realizes she is still wearing cat ears and takes them off with a playful 'Meow'.)

Please tell me it's my turn because I don't want to cross talk but –TADA! I met someone. He's sexy, he's hot, he's...my daughters' age. But listen, ladies, I am feeling a whole new vibration level here. I mean, he's adorable! He's an actor and a bartender so it's perfect!!! But he's so much more. He's smart and deep and did I say adorable? We talk for hours on the phone almost every night about life and the cosmos and our love for old movies but it goes by like that! *(She snaps her fingers.)* Okay, so he's a whole lotta young but...he gets me. I'm 'gotten'. And that's a first! Grrrrr!

[MUSIC: No. 9B – "CASABLANCA"]

Maybe there's hope for me after all.

(LILY sings and with each line, she morphs into a more confident woman.)

ON THE PROWL

(She begins to slip out of her coat.)

ON THE PROWL

(She strikes a sexy pose.)

ON THE PROWL

(Dragging her coat, she exits seductively.)

Scene Eleven. Fantasy Sequence at 'The Cats-ablanca Bar'

(The setting has the look and feel of a film noir, 1940's Sam Spade movie. BUCK stands with cigarette in hand and a bar towel over his shoulder. A saxophone wails in the distance.)

BUCK. *(a la Humphrey Bogart)* It was a cold, rainy night at the Cats-ablanca Bar. I was just a bartender/detective but I had one helluva'n itch...and then she walked in...

(LILY enters wearing a leopard print skirt over her Catwoman outfit and strikes a powerful feline pose.)

LILY. *(a la Lauren Bacall)* I'm looking for a hunk of flesh to devour!

BUCK. She was a glamour puss alright. And I could tell she had plenty of sc-r-r-ratch!

LILY. I sashayed in and curled up on the stool. It was dark and smoky just like I like it...the kind of lighting that gives a lady a lift, if you know what I mean. I flashed a gam to a certain young buck who looked to be giving me the eye.

BUCK. She was worth a stare so I did, damn it! I gave the dame the eye.

(BUCK closes one eye while popping the other wide open towards LILY.)

Bonk!

LILY. Well...here's looking at you, kid!

BUCK. How about a glass of milk on the house?

LILY. You hit on all your customers?

BUCK. Only the ones wearing leopard print skirts.

LILY. Meow! Now, how about you go fetch me a Cougartini?

BUCK. What's a Cougartini?

(She addresses the audience as though she is doing a commercial.)

LILY. A Cougartini is a martini for the woman over forty. It's made with pomegranate juice and vanilla vodka so it has the anti-oxidants to keep you feeling young… and the vodka to help you forget…that you're not.

BUCK. I think your confidence is sexy.

LILY. And I like you cuz' you stay up late.

BUCK. You got an inner glow that could light up Times Square!

LILY. *(to the audience a la movie voiceover)* I could feel my knees start to buckle. I wanted to crawl into his lap while he was still standing.

BUCK. So why don't ya, cha-cha-cha?

(**BUCK** *sweeps her up and twirls her around. Lights change to reveal that we are actually in* **BUCK**'s *apartment.*)

LILY. Ooh, you're so spontaneous. And you have no nose or ear hair.

BUCK. Gee, thanks…

LILY. *(looking around)* And I like your shared sublet. What do you call the décor, "early slacker"?

BUCK. *(cracking up)* You're good, Cats-ablanca Woman.

LILY. And you…

(**LILY** *and* **BUCK** *look lovingly into each others eyes.*)

[MUSIC: No. 10 – "I'M EASY"]

LILY. *(slow and sexy)*

YOU ARE SO YOUNG, YOU ARE SO FINE
HOW WOULD I KNOW THIS HEART OF MINE
COULD MAKE ME FEEL SO EASY?

I'VE LOST MY WILL, I'VE LOST MY PRIDE
AND NOW THERE'S NOWHERE LEFT TO HIDE
I GUESS THAT I'M JUST EASY

I ADMIT I INDULGE ALL MY SENSES
WHEN YOU GIVE ME YOUR STIFF… UPPER HAND

AND I JUST GOTTA SPEAK, IT FEELS STRONG TO BE WEAK

WHEN YOU'RE PLAYING IN WONDERLAND

UNDER THE SHEETS, UNDER THE SKIES
YOU'VE TOUCHED MY HEART, MY HEAD... MY THIGHS
AND I WILL BE SO EASY

YOU SHOULD KNOW THAT THERE'S NO TURNING
    BACKWARDS...
UNLESS YOU'D LIKE TO GIVE IT A TRY

PLEASE DON'T LAUGH IF I WEEP, IT'S JUST I'VE HAD NO
    SLEEP
BUT THEY'RE HAPPY TEARS THAT I CRY

WHO CAN DENY, WHO CAN RESIST
THIS AGELESS, BONDING, FONDLING TRYST?
IT'S SO HARD, SO VERY...

(**BUCK** *presses up against her.*)

HARD,
TO NOT TO BE EASY!

(*As lights fade to black, they kiss passionately.*)

[MUSIC: No. 10A – "APPLAUSE SEGUE"]

Scene Twelve. The Elder Grille and
Younger Boys Lounge

(MARY-MARIE *is at the bar looking at her laptop.*
CLARITY *is taking notes.*)

MARY-MARIE. Clarity, come take a look at my online membership services. Let's see here, I have blocked off Bourbon Cowboy.

CLARITY. I should think so.

MARY-MARIE. Oh, and I got an 'interview' in a little while with a tasty little tidbit named Peter who said, 'I want to meet you naked to represent the honesty of my soul'. Isn't that beautiful?

CLARITY. Naked! You're not seriously considering doing that, are you?

MARY-MARIE. Clarity, I am so ready to expose my inner being. And clothes, what are they but a metaphor for covering up one's true essence?

CLARITY. Donna Karan would not agree. Besides, Mary-Marie, get real. Clothes keep you warm and protect you from the cold!

MARY-MARIE. I do not live in the Tundra. Oh, and lookie here! Goliath wrote to me and said, 'Dear Miss Kitty, I believe in puttin' my woman, regardless of her age, on a pedestal and livin' to serve my Beloved Queen.'

CLARITY. Beloved Queen? Let me see that! Hmmm, and he has a masters in Global Studies! Would you mind if I were to contact this young man...for research purposes.

MARY-MARIE. Sure, have at it, Miss Clarity. As a matter of fact, I double-booked myself today and was supposed to meet Goliath for a first look-see at Starbucks. Why don't you go in my stead?

CLARITY. Well, perhaps I will! Let me take his number down and apprise him that I should like to get into his head and see what makes him tick.

(CLARITY starts dialing his number into her phone.)

MARY-MARIE. You are such a devoted student. And now, if you'll excuse me, I need to prepare for my meeting with 'Naked Peter'.

CLARITY. I'll be back later. Don't get pneumonia.

MARY-MARIE. Au revoir!

CLARITY. *(into her phone)* Is this Goliath? Hi. You don't know me. My name is…

(CLARITY exits, not realizing she has left her notebook on the bar.)

MARY-MARIE. Wait, Clarity! You forgot your notebook!

(The bar phone rings. MARY-MARIE answers.)

Miss Kitty… Oh, hello, Frank, it's you again. Yes, I got your five voice mails. The Symphony at Carnegie Hall? Black Tie? Champagne and dancing with P. Diddy? Uh, you know that sounds wonderful but I have an important staff meetin' that evenin'. Work, work, work! But I daresay, thank you for thinkin' of me. OK, bye. *(She hangs up slowly.)* Hmmm…that sounds good. Nah!

(Fade to black as she exits.)

[MUSIC: No. 10B – "GOLIATH INTRO"]

Scene Thirteen. Starbucks

(As the "Julio" theme plays, CLARITY crosses in a businesslike manner and checks her phone for directions. At Starbucks, GOLIATH, a handsome, well-dressed, young man is putting two cups of designer coffee on a table. He strikes a stylish, confident pose. CLARITY walks in, looks around and spots him.)

CLARITY. *(extending her hand)* You must be Goliath.

GOLIATH. *(a la Antonio Banderas)* And you must be Clarity

(They shake hands and sit down.)

So much more beautiful than I even imagined.

CLARITY. *(blushing in spite of herself)* Oh! Very nice to meet you too.

GOLIATH. Caramel Machiatto, eh?

CLARITY. Thank you! *(back to business)* I was fascinated by your profile on Cougar Life.

GOLIATH. Thank you, *fair maiden.*

(CLARITY reacts, in spite of herself.)

I was so intrigued when you called. I've been yearning to meet a regal lady who is powerful, and strong and educated.

CLARITY. *(checking him out)* And it's nice to finally meet a young man who's not wearing '*butt-crack*' jeans!

(She laughs at her own joke – in spite of herself.)

GOLIATH. Ah, you are not only beautiful and generous but you have a sense of humor. I like that.

(They look at each other tango-style, and then look front in unison.)

Would you be interested in taking this conversation a little further? Perhaps, we could venture to a bar that I own adjacent to my Jimmy Choo Store.

CLARITY. Jimmy Choo Store? I'm a glutton for shoes.

GOLIATH. I noticed... 9B?

CLARITY. Wow.

GOLIATH. It's just a small investment I dabble in to mix up my active portfolio as an independent venture capitalist.

CLARITY. You are a very diverse guy. I should be taking notes…

(She reaches into her briefcase and picks up a small pad. **GOLIATH** *extends his pen to her with great pomp and circumstance.)*

GOLIATH. Please, use my Zero Gravity Stylo. Well, my tastes range from the simple to the profound. I like to have breakfast on the balcony of La Casa Que Canta but I'm equally happy flipping burgers on the Barbie in stone washed jeans. I'm also a Four Star organic chef…

(She looks at him in amazement.)

Just a hobby. How does fresh-grilled snapper with jasmine rice and green tea foam sound on your pallet?

CLARITY. *(mesmerized)* Sounds delicious. I never had foam… *on my pallet.*

GOLIATH. I love to watch chick flicks and I enjoy discussing feelings that come up after a good tearjerker. I'm strong enough in my manhood to allow you to be the alpha woman you were meant to be. Is that a problem?

CLARITY. Do you recycle?

GOLIATH. I do. Zone 5. Our planet needs the help.

(He seductively takes the pen out of her fingers.)

And now, that I sense our synergy is real, I must confess "Goliath" is merely a screen name.

CLARITY. No…

GOLIATH. Yes. My real name is… Julio.

[MUSIC: No. 10C – "GOLIATH OUTRO"]

*(**CLARITY** does a 'take' to the audience and throws her notepad into the wings. **JULIO** stands and offers her his hand, pulling her into a standing position. They salsa out of Starbucks to the "Julio" theme. **CLARITY** whoops with abandon.)*

Scene Fourteen. Mary-Marie's Office/"Boudoir"

(MARY-MARIE enters and sits on the chaise lounge while putting on brand new, sexy pumps.)

MARY-MARIE. I just love interviews. Now, let me control the scene. *(She stands up and starts strategically planning the upcoming event.)* I'll set the screen here. Naked Peter will come in from over there. I will conceal myself behind the screen and then at the right moment, that shall be determined by *my* libido, we will both reveal our nakedness! *(looking skyward)* Henry Senior, just look at your shy Mary-Marie now!

(She rolls a pink dressing screen out from the wing. Her sweet, little, Southern-girl demeanor changes into a hard, bawdy stripper a la Mae West.)

[MUSIC: No. 11 – "MY TERMS"]

COME ON OVER TO MY HOUSE
LEAVE YOUR CLOTHES BY THE DOOR.
MAMA'S GONNA TAKE CARE OF YOU
SHOW ME SUMPIN', I'LL SHOW YOU MORE

(She struts out from behind the screen and struggles to remove her blouse, finally revealing a purple bustier underneath.)

A GLASS OF WINE, SOME BUBBLY
PERHAPS A SCOTCH ON ICE
COULD MAKE YOU FEEL REAL CUDDLY
AND THAT WOULD BE SO NICE

WE'LL DO IT ON MY TERMS, ON MY DIME
IT KEEPS THINGS NICE AND NEAT
IF IT'S MY TERMS YOU FOLLOW
I MIGHT MASSAGE YOUR FEET!

(She pulses her hips, pounding one of her new heels into the floor.)

Ow! These damn shoes!

(She hobbles to the chaise lounge and adjusts her shoes. She looks down at her bustier.)

What the hell is going on in here?

(She begins to adjust her breasts.)

Mary-Marie, just don't come on too strong this time!

(She switches back to her Mae West persona.)

I KNOW WHEN IT'S TIME
TO GET SOME ACTION
I KEEP MYSELF IN A POSITIVE MIND
CUZ THAT'S THE LAW OF ATTRACTION

WHEN I WAS YOUNG I WAS SO FOOLISH
GUIDED BY MY HEART
I COULDN'T FIND MY G-SPOT
SO THAT'S THE PLACE TO START!

LET'S DO IT ON MY TERMS
ON MY DIME, NO NEED TO KISS AND TELL
IF IT'S MY TERMS WE FOLLOW
WE'LL GIT ALONG REAL SWELL!

(She struts across the stage, dragging the screen behind her and trips. She recovers and continues her stripper routine.)

THE ANSWERS LIE WITHIN- SO WE SHOULD NOW LAY DOWN, MY BOY
NO MATTER WHERE YOU BEEN, I'LL MAKE YOU HOWL AND SCREAM WITH JOY
I'M PLAYIN' TO WIN AND I'LL MAKE YOU MY NEW BOY TOY

AS LONG AS YOU'RE YOUNG, AND REALLY WELL HUNG
YOU CAN BE A MUSLIM, A JEW OR A GOY, OY- OY-OY-OY!!!!!!!!!

(She struggles with the clasp of her flowing skirt until she gets it off. Then she coyly uses it (a la Gypsy Rose Lee) to hide herself, and slips behind the screen for her final reveal.)

LET'S DO IT ON MY TERMS
NOW NOTHING'S RIGHT OR WRONG

(She slips off the bustier and places it over the screen, giving the impression that she is now naked.)

CUZ IT'S MY TERMS WE'LL FOLLOW
YEAH, MY RULES ALL NIGHT LONG

IT'S MY TERMS, IT'S MY DIME
BABY, DON'T BE CRUEL *(a la Elvis)*

(She puts on a flimsy robe.)

WHEN IT'S MY TERMS YOU FOLLOW

(On stripper drum riff, she struts out from behind the screen and strikes a pose.)

CUZ YOU'RE AT COUGAR SCHOOL!

(Giggling at her own audacity, she moves the screen center stage, perpendicular to audience, dividing stage right and stage left.)

[MUSIC: No. 11A – "MY TERMS PLAYOFF"]

MARY-MARIE. My highest good now comes to pass, as I trust the process of life!

*(**NAKED PETER** appears in silhouette in the upstage doorway. He is wearing a trench coat, black shoes and socks, with a fedora pulled low over his face.)*

MARY-MARIE. Step right on in, Naked Peter! Yaow! I am the mastress of your destiny, tonight!

*(**NAKED PETER** sashays downstage to his side of the screen as lights dim.)*

MARY-MARIE. Count down to ecstasy, three... two... one... Go!

*(They step out from behind the screen and flash each other in unison without the audience seeing the 'goods'. **NAKED PETER** squints, and juts his chin forward.)*

NAKED PETER. Mom?

MARY-MARIE. *(screaming)* Ahhhhhhhhh!

*(**MARY-MARIE** closes her robe. **HENRY JUNIOR**, aka **NAKED PETER**, closes his coat, mortified. Blackout)*

Scene Fifteen. The Park

(LILY and CLARITY are sitting on a bench. CLARITY holds a small note pad.)

CLARITY. *(dreamily)* So isn't sex great with a younger man?

LILY. What?

CLARITY. *(snapping out of it)* What? What? I mean, what's sex like with a younger man?

LILY. It's glorious. It's like the world is deep and wide. But you know, Buck doesn't feel younger to me. He just feels good. But, we did make out in front of the 'Madonna and Child' when we went to the Met.

CLARITY. Glad to see that life is imitating art.

(LILY looks at her, quizzically.)

So… when do you plan to pull the plug on this guy?

LILY. What? I don't have a plan. I mean, I'm just saying YES to life like you told me to. And wish I had done it sooner! The burden I carried about never measuring up, the regret about not having my Dad's approval, the Garys, the shame…it's gone. I'm finally free!

CLARITY. You do seem happier. I'll give you that.

LILY. Yeah, I've never felt this way before! I can't wait for you to get Buck's take on this.

(LILY's cell phone rings. The ring tone is "Somewhere Over the Rainbow".)

Mary-Marie? Slow down. Whoa, what? I can't understand a word you're saying, honey. Listen, okay, okay, I'll be right there.

(She hangs up.)

CLARITY. What's going on?

LILY. Mary-Marie is having some sort of emergency. I better go. *(LILY starts to go.)* Tell Buck I'll text him.

CLARITY. Okay. Let me know if there's anything I can do.

LILY. Okay, bye.

*(**LILY** exits. **CLARITY**'s cell phone rings. The ring tone is a fun salsa.)*

CLARITY. Hello, you. Me, too! I can't stop thinking of green tea foam on my palate. See you soon. I'll bring the wine.

*(**BUCK** enters. **CLARITY** hangs up quickly and grabs her note pad.)*

Hello, Buck!

BUCK. Hello, 'Thesis Lady'!

(He sits down beside her.)

CLARITY. Thank you, so much for coming to meet with me. I'm glad to finally get your point of view. So tell me, "Why?"

BUCK. 'Why' what?

CLARITY. Other than sex…why?

(Underscore of "It's Hard to Not Be Easy" begins.)

BUCK. I dunno. I've never felt like this before. It's just happening to me. She's not asking for anything except my company, which is cool. And when we laugh, her eyes crinkle and she glows with this happiness. She may be older but for the first time I feel like…a man.

CLARITY. I see.

*(As lights cross fade, we hear **MARY-MARIE** wail.)*

Scene Sixteen. Elder Grille and Younger Boys Lounge

(MARY-MARIE enters, a soused, disheveled mess, holding a bottle of Jack Daniels in one hand and a glass in the other.)

MARY-MARIE. Oh, dear God! I'm a horrible mother! I can't believe I ever did that to my child! There's no affirmation that can help with this predicament.

(She pours a drink but swigs from the bottle instead.)

Oh, Henry Junior, please forgive me! I never knew you were *dabblin'!*

(She drinks from the glass as the bar phone rings. She tries to steady herself as she drunkenly walks to the phone.)

Hello? Oh Frank…I've been better. I'm havin' some *mama drama* in my life. What did you just say? "We are always perfect, whole and complete"? *(She chokes up.)* Why, thank you! Bye.

(LILY comes running in.)

LILY. Mary-Marie, are you OK?

MARY-MARIE. Oh Lily, I'm so glad you're here. I'm such an asshole! My life is over. Take me now, Lord!

(MARY-MARIE raises her arms to the sky with drink in one hand and bottle in the other.)

LILY. What happened, sweetie?

MARY-MARIE. HENRY JUNIOR is NAKED PETER!

LILY. What?

MARY-MARIE. I came on to my own son! Although, I didn't know he was my son. I thought he was *Naked-Peter's-mother's son*. Oh, that poor boy, he's been through so much and now…an *Oedipus complex!*

LILY. But wait, he contacted *you* online, yes?

MARY-MARIE. Uh, huh…

LILY. And you had no idea he was Henry Junior, right?

MARY-MARIE. Uh, huh…

LILY. That's so odd. Don't you have to show a picture?

MARY-MARIE. I met him on Craigslist.

LILY. What? Are you nuts?

MARY-MARIE. I'm so embarrassed.

LILY. *(changing tack)* Honey, it was an accident. Just learn from your *(under her breath) extreme lack of judgment.*

> **(MARY-MARIE** *howls.)*

Listen, "There are no mistakes, everything happens for a reason." Okay, look, Henry Junior may need a therapy session or two –

MARY-MARIE. Or a hundred!

LILY. -but in the scheme of things both he and you will be Okay. Come on, honey, let me take that bottle out of your hand.

> **(LILY** *pries the bottle out of* **MARY-MARIE***'s resistant hand.)*

MARY-MARIE. At least, I hold my liquor good. It's just Henry Junior and I haven't spoken for the last six months, per his request, so he could go "find himself" and now *(sudden realization)* he's seen my VA-JAY-JAY!

LILY. Mary-Marie, this is the time to go within your feisty Southern Spirit and *walk the talk y'all been spewing forth!*

MARY-MARIE. Oh honey, I suppose you're right. *(She blows her nose with her robe.)* I reckon we'll all be laughin' about this in a *thousand years*. Wait! Maybe somewhere on the planet, exposin' yourself to your son is a good thing… a rite of passage, like pushing the baby bird out of the nest to fly!

LILY. *(doubtfully)* Uh…right.

MARY-MARIE. *(poignantly)* Y'know, when Henry Junior was a baby, he had the cutest little chubby cheeks. And these blue eyes that would dance all around the room. But when he'd lock in on mine, everything stood still. I was like the sun and the moon and the stars, all wrapped up in one. *(Musical underscore.)* And cuz I was his Mama, I didn't need no affirmation. I miss my boy. I just wish I could tuck him in one more time.

[MUSIC: No. 12 – "A MOTHER'S LOVE"]

HUSH MY LITTLE HENRY DON'T YOU CRY
MAMA'S GONNA KISS YOUR TEARS GOODBYE
MAMA'S GONNA HOLD YOU OH SO TIGHT
MAMA'S GONNA MAKE YOU SAFE TONIGHT

SEEMS LIKE YESTERDAY YOU WERE A TOT
ONLY TOOK A HUG TO SMILE A LOT
ONLY TOOK A NAP TO GIVE YOU REST

MARY-MARIE/LILY.

ONLY TOOK YOUR MOM TO LOVE YOU BEST

MARY-MARIE.

I CAN'T EXPRESS THE WAY I FEEL
I PINCHED MYSELF, WAS THIS FOR REAL?

LILY.

THE DAY THEY CAME INTO MY WORLD
THEY CHANGED MY LIFE, MY SPECIAL LITTLE GIRLS

MARY-MARIE/LILY.

AS WE ALL GROW OLDER YOU SHOULD KNOW
LIFE, IT CAN BE HARD, GO WITH THE FLOW
AND WHEN YOUR BABIES CRY MAYBE YOU WILL HEAR
THE LULLABY I SANG IN YOUR EAR

MARY-MARIE.

THE WORDS DON'T COME SO EASILY

MARY-MARIE/LILY.

THEY CAN'T COMPARE TO THE LOVE IN ME

LILY.

I LOOK AT YOU, MY HEART STANDS STILL

MARY-MARIE/LILY.

THOUGH YOU MAY CHANGE, IT NEVER WILL
I COULD NEVER THANK YOU ENOUGH
FOR GIVING ME

MARY-MARIE.

A MOTHER'S LOVE

LILY.

A MOTHER'S LOVE

MARY-MARIE/LILY.

> A MOTHER'S LOVE
> HUSH MY LITTLE BABY, DON'T YOU...
>
> *(The bar phone rings.* **LILY** *picks it up and hands the receiver to* **MARY-MARIE.***)*

MARY-MARIE. Oh, Henry Junior, I'm so glad you called.

> *(***LILY** *moves away to give her some privacy.)*
>
> What? Oh, thank God! *(She covers the receiver.)* He said he didn't have his contacts in so it was *all a blur*! *(into the phone)* Oh, honey, I love you, too. Yes, let's talk tomorrow. Bye, bye. *(She jumps for joy as she hangs up the phone.)* Oh, my highest good DOES come to pass!

LILY. Guess what doesn't kill you makes you stronger!

> *(They hug and heave a deep sigh of relief, in unison.* **LILY** *spots* **CLARITY***'s notebook on the bar.)*
>
> Hey, what's that?

MARY-MARIE. Oh, Clarity forgot her notebook. By the way, she said I was the *star* of her thesis.

LILY. I bet you are. She wouldn't mind if I took a sneak peak, would she?

MARY-MARIE. No, go ahead!

> *(***LILY** *opens the notebook and begins to read.)*

LILY. OK. 'A prime example of the Cougar phenomenon is a gal who I'll refer to as *Miss Kitty*...'

MARY-MARIE. See, this is it!

LILY. '...who pays for love in any vapid way she can get it, specifically with younger men who are only too eager for her hand-outs.'

MARY-MARIE. What? Let me see that. *(grabs the notebook)* Holy shit, I been Shanghai-ed! 'Another example of low self esteem is a woman who I will refer to as 'L' who never got over feeling abandoned by her father.'

LILY. What the fu –

> *(A slightly tousled* **CLARITY** *appears at the doorway, bidding an amorous adieu to an offstage* **JULIO.***)*

CLARITY. Buenos noches, mi amor, I shall meet you later!

(She blows him a kiss and salsas toward the ladies, singing a la Paul Simon)

"ME AND JULIO DOWN BY THE SCHOOL YARD". Oh, ladies, I had the most divine time. Ole!

*(**LILY** holds out the notebook.)*

Oh no!

MARY-MARIE. I am speechless, unusually speechless. I mean, I don't know what to say, it's like I can't even put two words together, I'm –

CLARITY. Look, I can explain.

LILY. Here.

*(She hands **CLARITY** the notebook.)*

You might wanna take notes. I thought you liked us. All along you were judging us?

MARY-MARIE. And our lifestyle. I'm speechless –

CLARITY. Wait!

LILY. I say you're two-faced and manipulative – acting all high and mighty like you're above it all when what's really going on is you are too afraid to let anyone in. I might be insecure but at least I'm not a coward!

CLARITY. Well, who do you think YOU are reading my private notes? I feel violated.

LILY. I feel violated!

MARY MARIE. I feel violated!

CLARITY. Look, I had to support my original thesis statement and find examples to prove my theory and you girls were the perfect specimens.

LILY/MARY MARIE. Specimens?

CLARITY. No! No, I mean, something just happened with this man I met. One minute I'm in control, ready to take notes and the next minute, I don't know what happened! But, wow, ironically for the first time in 20 years, I found myself feeling beautiful in front of a prince of a man and desiring him. And age had nothing to do with it!

LILY. Oh, please.

CLARITY. OK, alright, maybe I did walk in here feeling a little superior. But now I see that strong women come in many different forms. I'm sorry.

LILY. Gee, you think it's that simple? You say you're sorry and it's over?

MARY-MARIE. It worked for David Letterman.

LILY. I trusted you and you betrayed me!

CLARITY. You're right. I'm so sorry.

MARY-MARIE. See, she apologized.

LILY. *(not buying it)* But hell, I get it now. I've crossed the U-Bend. Because your opinion of me is not my opinion of me cuz I happen to think a lot of me and Buck and I don't care what you think, I love him. Did I just say that?

MARY-MARIE. Oh my God, this is serious!

LILY. Did I just say that?

CLARITY. Yes and I get it now!

MARY-MARIE. She gets it now!

LILY. Oh my God, I have to tell Buck I love him!

MARY-MARIE. Well, you go, girl!

CLARITY. Go for it!

LILY. Thanks, ladies!

(LILY exits.)

MARY-MARIE. Ooowhee, what a day!

CLARITY. You can say that again.

MARY MARIE. What a day. So tell me, what happened with Goliath? Did you get slayed?

CLARITY. Oh, he's amazing and very evolved.

MARY-MARIE. Well, honey, I reckon you're gonna have to rewrite your thesis now.

CLARITY. Omigod…I'm a Cougar!

(Blackout)

[MUSIC: No. 12A – "INTRO TO AGELESS"]

Scene Seventeen. The Park

(Underscore of "I'm Easy". **LILY** *rushes in.* **BUCK** *is waiting for her on the park bench.)*

LILY. Hey!

BUCK. Hey, there you are!

(They embrace.)

LILY. *(breathless)* Oh Buck, I –

BUCK. – I have something to tell you!

LILY. Me too!

LILY AND BUCK. *(simultaneously)* So I –

(They laugh.)

You go first!

LILY. It's okay, you can go.

BUCK. Cool. Well, because of you, I've been doing a lot of soul searching.

LILY. That's great!

BUCK. Yeah, and I don't want to be an actor anymore. I mean, I wanted to be Kevin Bacon after I saw *Footloose* but since I met you I want to be...me, contribute to the world in a big way. I want to make a difference. And so, I'm going back to school to become *(proudly)...* a lawyer!

LILY. *(taken aback)* A lawyer? Wow... from the bar to the Bar!

BUCK. Cool, huh? I reapplied to Berkeley Law School and I got in. And it's all because of you.

LILY. Me? Wow. Why didn't you tell me before now?

BUCK. I wanted to surprise you.

LILY. Mission accomplished. Yikes. Berkeley. That's kinda far. When do you leave?

BUCK. Soon, like four weeks. Well, I gotta get cracking. Find a job, place to live, buy a car... it's not like New York, you know. *(He takes a moment and then springs it on her.)* And *you* are coming with me.

LILY. Coming with you?

BUCK. *(earnestly)* Why not? Think about it. Your kids are practically on their own. I have enough miles in my Jet Blue account to get you a one way ticket! Listen, all you have to do is pack your stuff and we are so out of here!

LILY. Oh, Buck! Sweet, sweet, spontaneous, Buck. It's not that easy...

BUCK. Sure, it is.

LILY. I just can't pick up and go.

BUCK. Why not? You can have, do or be anything if that's what you want? Right?

LILY. I want...I want what's best for you. Buck, you're starting on a whole new chapter in your life. I'd hold you back. I can't do that.

BUCK. *(after a beat)* Okay...so I won't go.

LILY. What do you mean?

BUCK. I can't leave you.

LILY. Of course, you can! Go on now. You have to get cracking. Find a job, place to live, buy a car– it's not like New York, you know.

BUCK. But I thought we –

LILY. *(tender but firm)* Buck, you're going to be so, so incredibly successful. You're going to shake up the world and raise the vibration level of this whole planet! I can just see the sign now: "Buck Forman, Esquire." But, hey, you'll always be my Buck.

BUCK. And you'll always be my... Cats-ablanca woman.

[MUSIC: No. 13 – "LOVE IS AGELESS"]

HOW OLD DOES A HEART HAVE TO BE TO REALLY FEEL?

AT WHAT AGE CAN YOU KNOW IN YOUR SOUL, IT'S FOR REAL?

WHEN I WAS JUST A BABY I COULD FEEL THINGS, IT WAS STRONG

IT WASN'T JUST LIKE MAYBE, I COULD FEEL IT RIGHT OR WRONG

AND IT'S TRUE I'M TELLING YOU

LILY.

> AND NOW AS I GAZE IN YOUR BEAUTIFUL EYES I FEEL
> WONDER
> IT'S SUCH A TENDER SURPRISE THAT THIS HUNGER FEELS
> RIGHT FOR ME
> AND LATELY, I AM WISER AND SO STRONG
> YOUR LOVE HAS TOUCHED ME GREATLY

BUCK.

> YOU HAVE MOVED ME ALL NIGHT LONG

BOTH.

> AND IT'S TRUE I'M TELLING YOU, MY LOVE IS AGELESS

LILY.

> IT COMES AS A SURPRISE. THE MORE I SEE YOU, THE MORE
> I REALIZE
> THIS HEART OF MINE, THIS MIND OF MINE
> TRULY WE ARE AGELESS.

BOTH.

> IT COMES AS A SURPRISE. THE MORE I SEE YOU, THE MORE
> I REALIZE
> THIS HEART OF MINE, THIS MIND OF MINE
> TRULY WE ARE AGELESS.
> TRULY LOVE IS AGELESS.

> *(They kiss passionately. She gently pushes him away. He
> reluctantly begins to leave.)*

LILY. Buck! *(He turns toward her.)* I love you.

BUCK. I love you, too.

> *(He blows her a kiss. She 'catches' it and places it on her
> heart. He exits, leaving* **LILY** *alone.)*

LILY. *(Singing softly)*

> MY LOVE IS AGELESS…

> *(She opens her hand and blows his kiss out into the
> universe. A star twinkles as piano tinkles. Slow fade to
> black)*

Scene Eighteen. In Limbo

[MUSIC: No. 13 – "EPILOGUE"]

("On The Prowl" vamp begins as **MARY-MARIE** *walks downstage into a special light. She is wearing a fringed cowboy jacket and cowboy hat.)*

MARY-MARIE. *(into her cell phone)* Hold on a second, darlin'. *(She covers the receiver and speaks to the audience.)* Well, I finally decided to give ol' Frank a call and I'm so glad I did because when I close my eyes and listen to him speak, he sounds so dang youthful. *(into the phone)* Frank, sweetie, I'll see you at 'The Palm' and don't forget your little blue pills, darlin'!

*(***MARY-MARIE*** exits right as* **CLARITY** *walks downstage into the special light.* **CLARITY** *is wearing glasses and a suit jacket.)*

CLARITY. Good morning class, and welcome to the Sacred Feminine Seminar! I am Professor Clarity Jackson. What do you call an older woman who is linked with a younger man? She's called…a WOMAN! Oh, and if you look in your folders, you will see that your scholarship to this course was funded by the Jimmy Choo Foundation.

*(***CLARITY*** exits left as* **BUCK** *walks downstage into the special. He is wearing a collegiate sweater.)*

BUCK. Well, I made it through law school and passed the bar. Decided to go into Entertainment Law. I figured it was a good fit, I mean, my love of movies and acting background made me a shoo-in candidate at the firm. They are fast tracking me for Partner. And speaking of partner, I'm engaged to a wonderful girl. After she said yes, the first phone call I made…was to Lily.

(As **BUCK** *exits left,* **LILY** *walks downstage into the special. "On the Prowl" vamp ends. She is wearing a jewel-toned, satin cocktail dress.)*

LILY. And now, I am in a relationship with the love of my life... ME! Yes!

(As **MARY-MARIE** *and* **CLARITY** *rush in to share a hug with* **LILY**, *lights cross fade, and we are in The Elder Grill and Younger Boys Lounge. Each of them is also wearing a jewel-toned cocktail dress. They move to the bar.)*

MARY-MARIE. Okay, girls! Last chance to get your Cougartini at the 'Grille and Boy'! I'm closin' the doors for renovation at midnight.

(She prepares three Cougartinis.)

CLARITY. Are you serious? I was gonna bring my class here for a field trip.

MARY-MARIE. Well, you can bring 'em to my new holistic, psychological, weight loss bar. Gonna call it, "Think, Drink and Shrink". *(She raises her glass.)* To the good times!

LILY AND CLARITY. *(toasting)* To the good times!

LILY. Hey, you know what Buck just texted me? "Inside the word COURAGE is the word COUGAR."

MARY-MARIE. Here's to courage!

CLARITY. Here's to stepping out of the kitty box!

LILY. Here's to friendship and to peace within!

MARY-MARIE. That's right, Dorothy, there is no place like
(intoning)
'OM'...

CLARITY. *(intoning a 3rd above)*
OM...

LILY. *(completing the chord)*
OM...

AT THE END OF THE DAY IT'S CLEAR,
MY COURAGE AND STRENGTH'S RIGHT HERE

MARY-MARIE.

I JUST DIDN'T KNOW THAT I HAD TO LET GO OF THE VOICE
OF LOSS AND FEAR

CLARITY.

> IN A SECOND, A MINUTE, AN HOUR, YOU'LL KNOW YOUR
>   HIDDEN POWER

ALL.

> THAT'S WHEN YOU FIND YOU WERE THERE ALL THE TIME.
> YOU ARE LOVE AT THE END OF THE DAY.

(Tempo accelerates.)

LILY.

> FOR SO LONG I'VE BEEN SEARCHING FOR FEELINGS OF
>   SAFETY AND PEACE

MARY-MARIE.

> I'VE BEEN TO THE BAR, TO THE CHURCH AND THE MALL
> AND STILL MY FRUSTRATION WOULDN'T CEASE

CLARITY.

> MAYBE I'D FIND THE ANSWERS IN THE NEXT BOOK OR NEXT
>   GOOD PLAY

ALL.

> OR IF I'D JUST BE GOOD AND DO WHAT A GIRL SHOULD
> EVERYTHING'D WORK OUT OK.
> BUT AT THE END OF THE DAY, IT'S CLEAR
> MY COURAGE AND STRENGTH'S RIGHT HERE
> I JUST DIDN'T KNOW THAT I HAD TO LET GO OF THE VOICE
>   OF LOSS AND FEAR
> IN A SECOND, A MINUTE, AN HOUR, YOU'LL KNOW YOUR
>   HIDDEN POWER
> THAT'S WHEN YOU FIND YOU WERE THERE ALL THE TIME
> YOU ARE LOVE AT THE END OF THE DAY.

LILY.

> I HAVE TRAVELED INTO MARRIAGE, TO DIVORCE AND NOW
>   I'M GAY
> Kidding!

CLARITY.

> LIFE COULDN'T GET ME DOWN, LONG AS I HAD MY CROWN
> LEAST THAT'S WHAT I HEARD MYSELF SAY

MARY-MARIE.

> MAYBE I'D FIND THE ANSWERS IN THE NEXT DATE OR NEXT
>   GOOD LAY

CLARITY.

NEXT GOOD LAY

(BUCK enters on the opposite side of stage, now a full-fledged lawyer dressed in a beautiful suit.)

LILY, MARY-MARIE, CLARITY AND BUCK.

IF I'D JUST HOLD ON TIGHT MAYBE SOME STARRY NIGHT
SOMETHING WOULD SHOW ME THE WAY

(Lights brighten to full stage. BUCK and the women join center.)

BUT AT THE END OF THE DAY, IT'S CLEAR
MY COURAGE AND STRENGTH'S RIGHT HERE
I JUST DIDN'T KNOW THAT I HAD TO LET GO OF THE
VOICE OF LOSS AND FEAR
IN A SECOND, A MINUTE, AN HOUR, YOU'LL KNOW YOUR
HIDDEN POWER
THAT'S WHEN YOU FIND YOU WERE THERE ALL THE
TIME.
YOU ARE LOVE AT THE END OF THE DAY

YOU ARE LOVE AT THE END OF THE DAY

YOU ARE LOVE AT THE END OF THE DAY!

(Blackout)

[MUSIC: No. 15 – "BOWS"]

End of Show

BOWS AND REPRISE

(instrumental)

ALL.

IN A SECOND, A MINUTE, AN HOUR, YOU'LL KNOW YOUR
    HIDDEN POWER
THAT'S WHEN YOU FIND YOU WERE THERE ALL THE TIME.
YOU ARE LOVE AT THE END OF THE DAY!
YOU ARE LOVE AT THE END OF THE DAY!
YOU ARE LOVE AT THE END OF THE DAY!

[MUSIC: No. 16 – "EXIT MUSIC"]